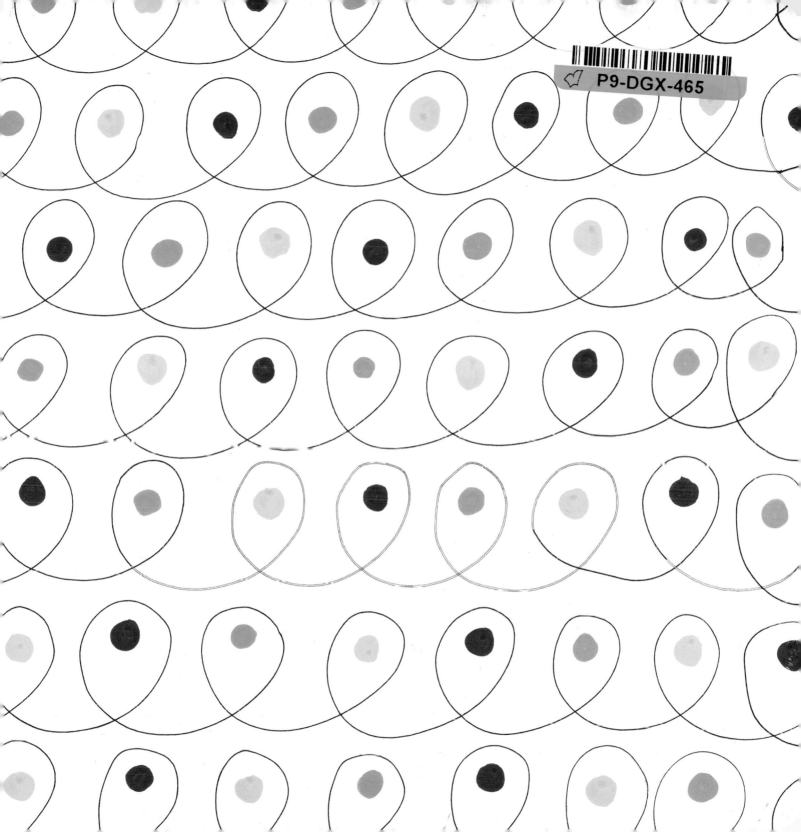

HEY THERE!
I'M GETTING A LITTLE BORED IN HERE.
WANNA PLAY?

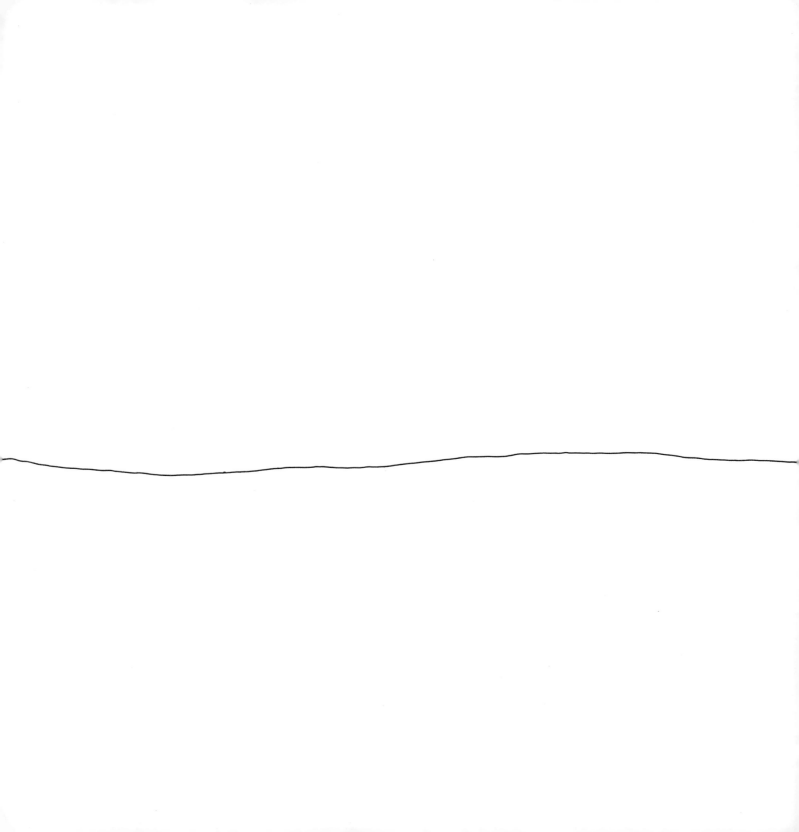

PRESS THE TOP CORNER TO GET ME STARTED.

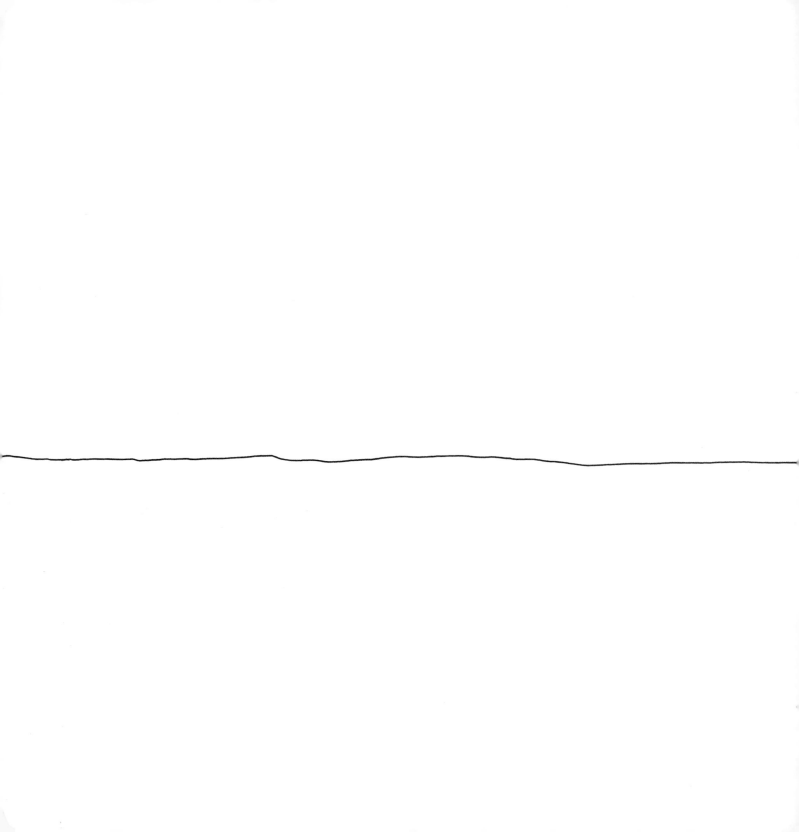

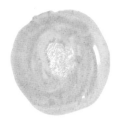

OK. NOW TRY THE BOTTOM CORNER . . .
YUP. DOWN THERE ON THE RIGHT.

GREAT! NOW LET'S GET BACK TO
THE MIDDLE OF THE PAGE . . .
GO ON, TRY IT.

THAT'S iT.
FEELS GOOD TO BE GETTING A BiT OF EXERCISE!

So, will you take me along?
It's easy: Just follow the line with your finger.

ALL RIGHT . . .
UP . . . DOWN . . . UP . . . DOWN . . . UP . . .

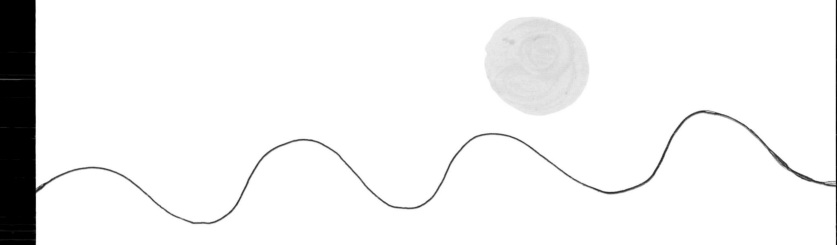

WHAT A HOOT!

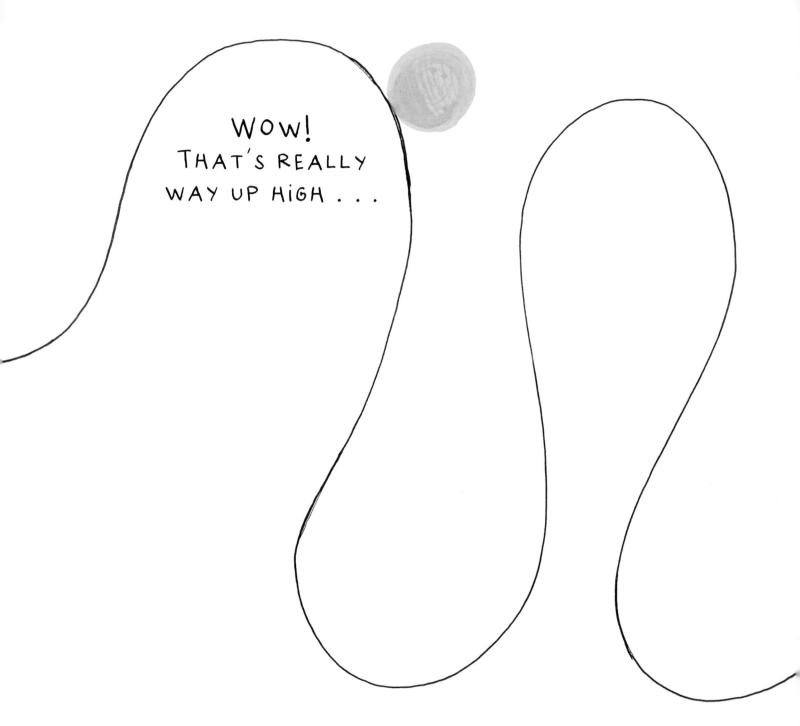

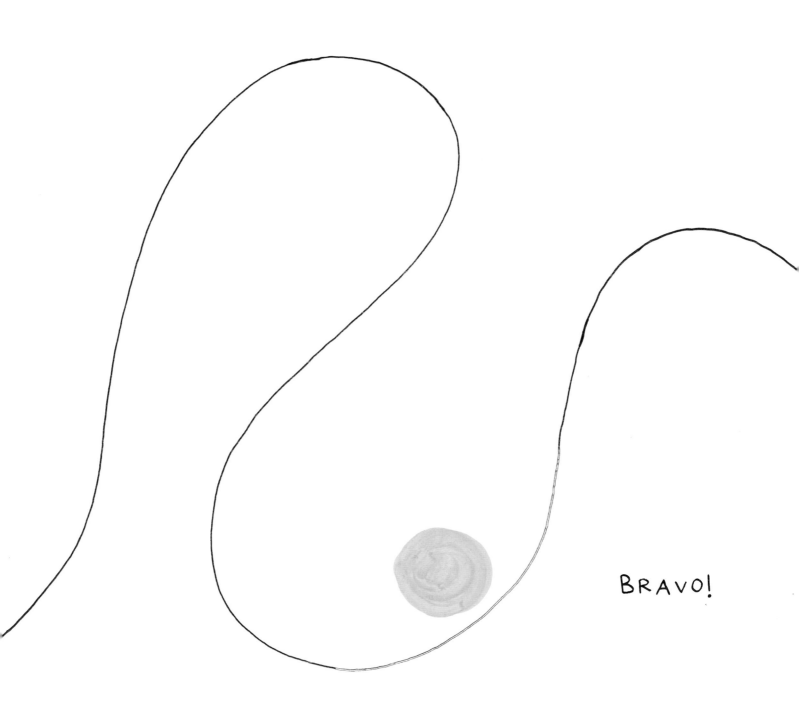

BRAVO!

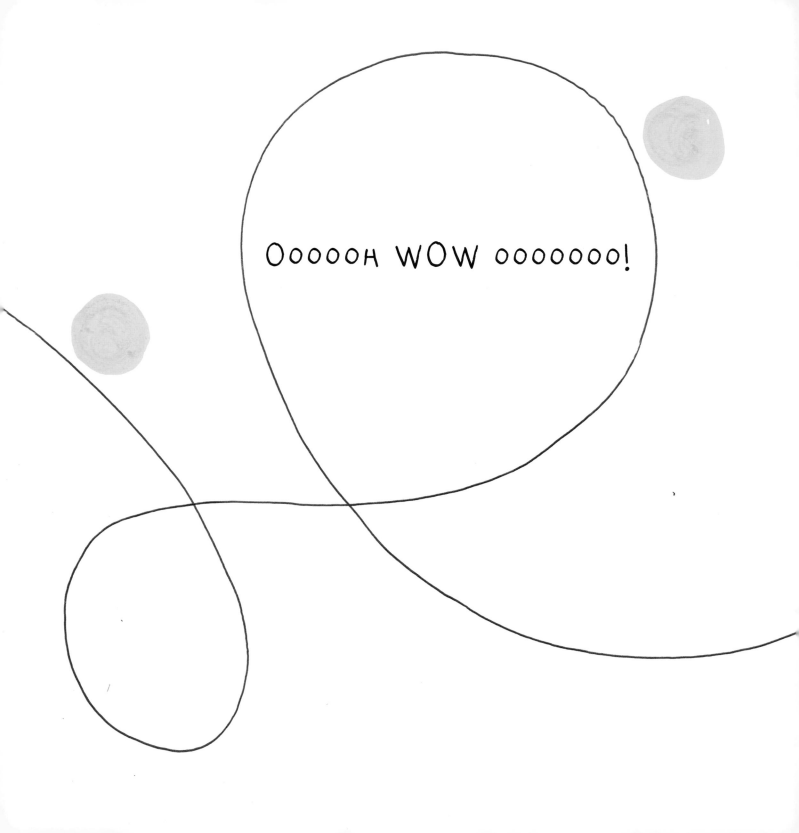

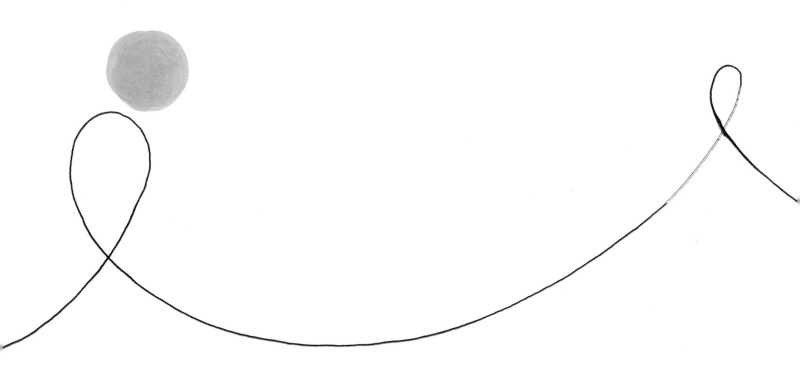

HEY, LOOK: A CAROUSEL!
WANT TO TAKE A SPIN?

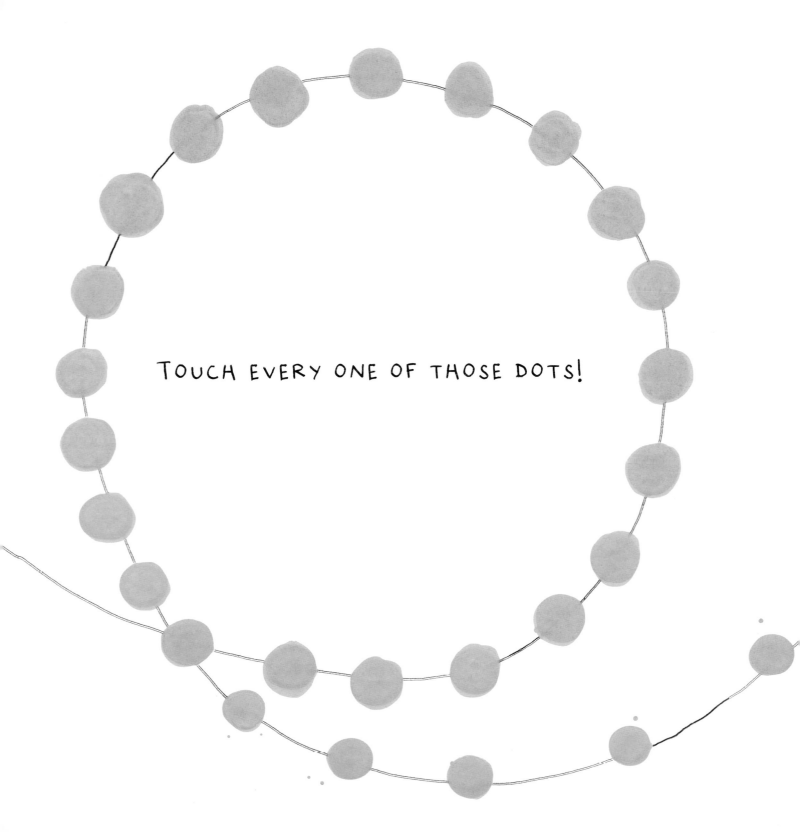

TOUCH EVERY ONE OF THOSE DOTS!

DID YOU SEE THAT?
YOU CHANGED ITS COLORS!

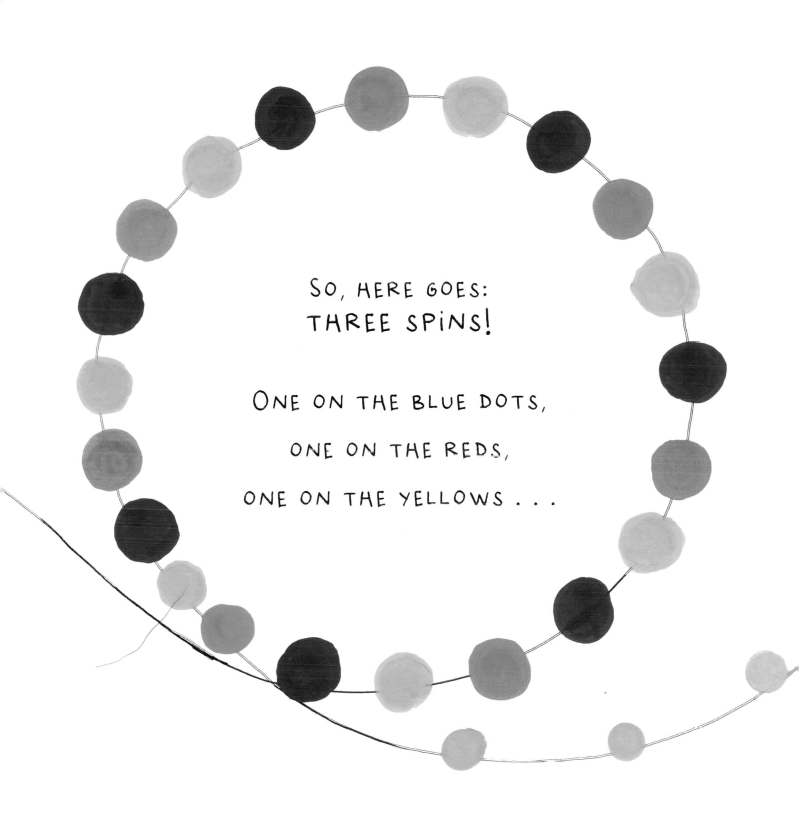

SO, HERE GOES:
THREE SPINS!

ONE ON THE BLUE DOTS,

ONE ON THE REDS,

ONE ON THE YELLOWS . . .

MAGNIFICENT!

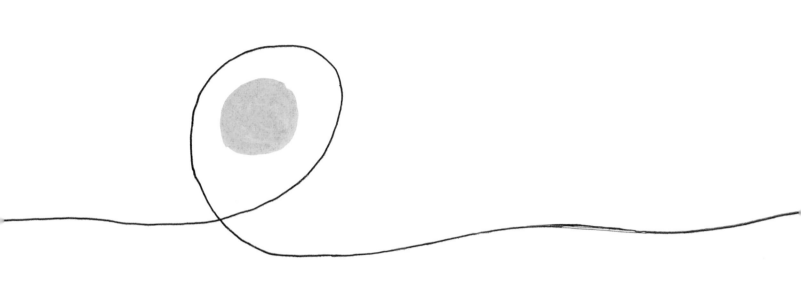

NOW WHAT DO YOU THINK WE SHOULD DO?

BRAVO!

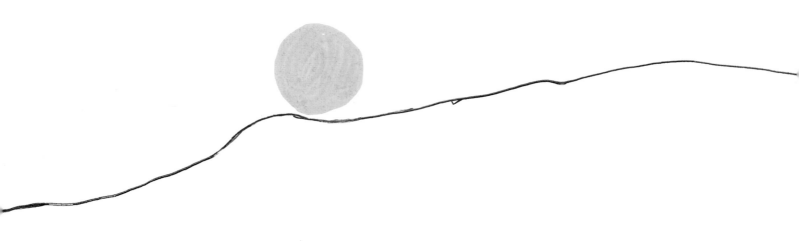

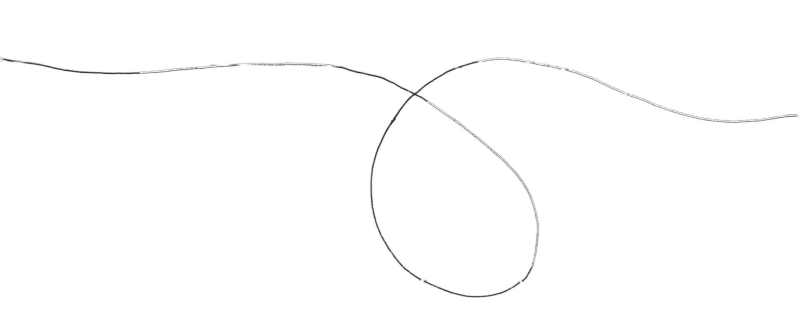

HEY! WHAT'S THAT OVER THERE?

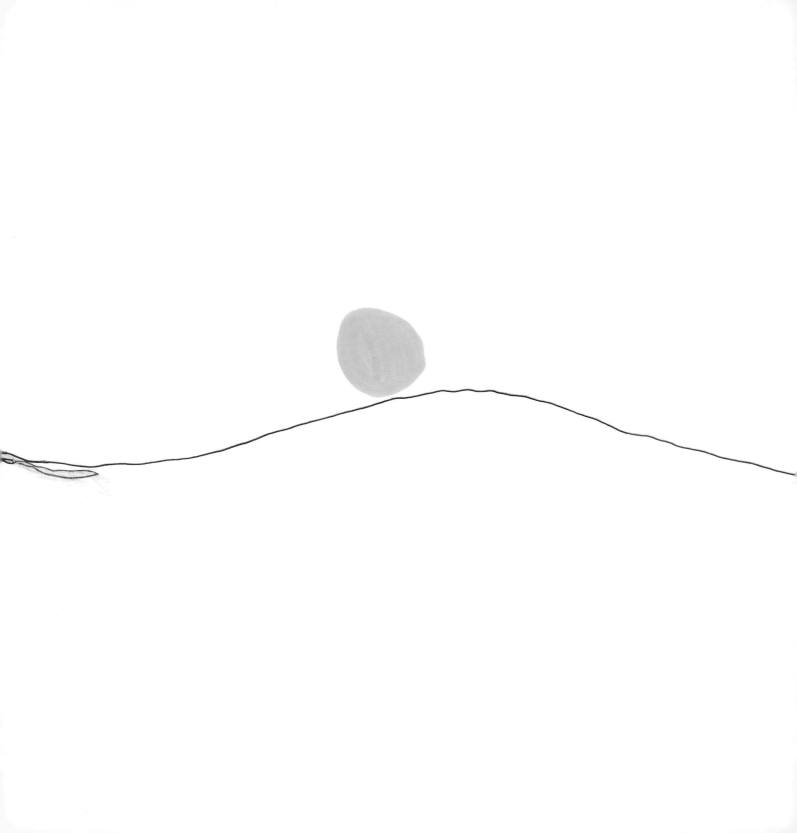

LET'S GO LOOK . . .
MAKE SURE YOU STICK TO THE LINE.

FOLLOW THOSE STAIRS.
THEY LEAD TO THE NEXT PAGE.

YOU CAN'T MAKE A SOUND . . . OK?

SHHHHHHHH . . .

Eeeek!
We better leave on tiptoe . . .

WHEW!

UH-OH . . . AAARGH . . . OUCH!
I DON'T WANT TO GO THROUGH THERE.
MAYBE I COULD JUST DISAPPEAR?

LET'S HOLD HANDS . . . CLOSE OUR EYES . . .

AND SAY ZA-ZA-ZOOMMM!

PHEW! THAT'S MUCH BETTER.
NOW YOU CAN MAKE ME REAPPEAR.

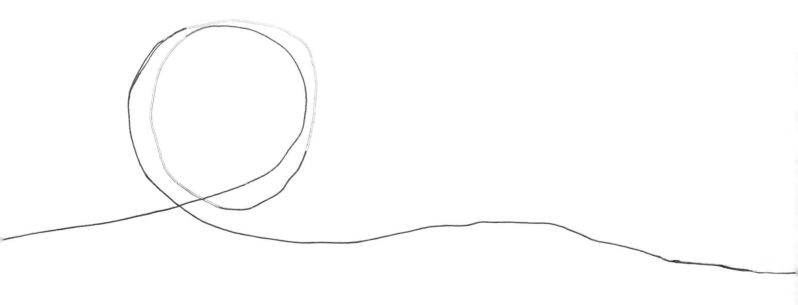

CLAP YOUR HANDS TWICE AND SAY ZA-ZA-ZOOMMM!
ZA-ZA-ZOOMMM! ZA-ZA-ZOOMMM!

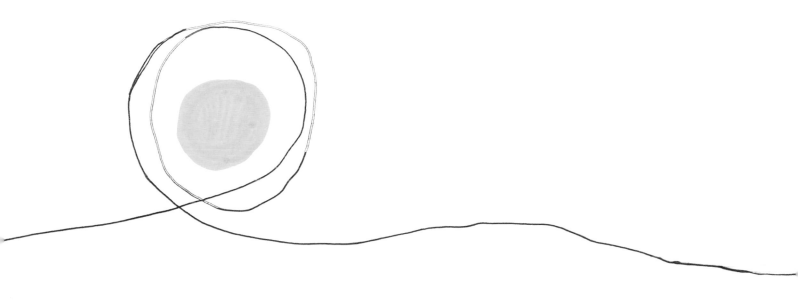

AHHH, THANK YOU!   NOW WE CAN GO ON . . .

UH-OH!

THERE'S SOMETHING UP AHEAD.
QUICK, TAKE YOUR FINGER AND
   PRESS ON ME REALLY HARD . . . AND THEN . . . LET GO!

ALMOST. TRY AGAIN.
PRESS REALLY, REALLY HARD . . . AND LET GO.

SO CLOSE.

ONE LAST TIME . . .
   PRESS . . . PRESS HARDER . . . LET GO.
      NOW BLOW REALLY HARD. YOU CAN DO IT!

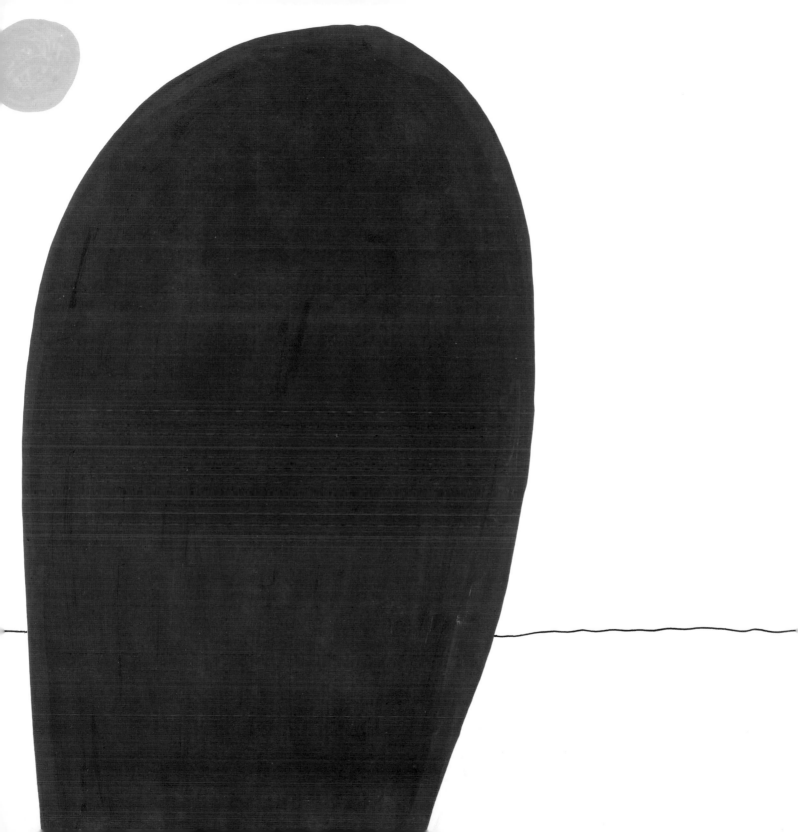

YOU DID IT! COOL.

YOO-HOO! CAN'T YOU SEE ME?
I'M RIGHT HERE ON TOP OF YOUR HEAD! AMAZING, RIGHT?

NOW LET ME GET OUT OF YOUR HAIR AND
BACK IN THE BOOK . . .

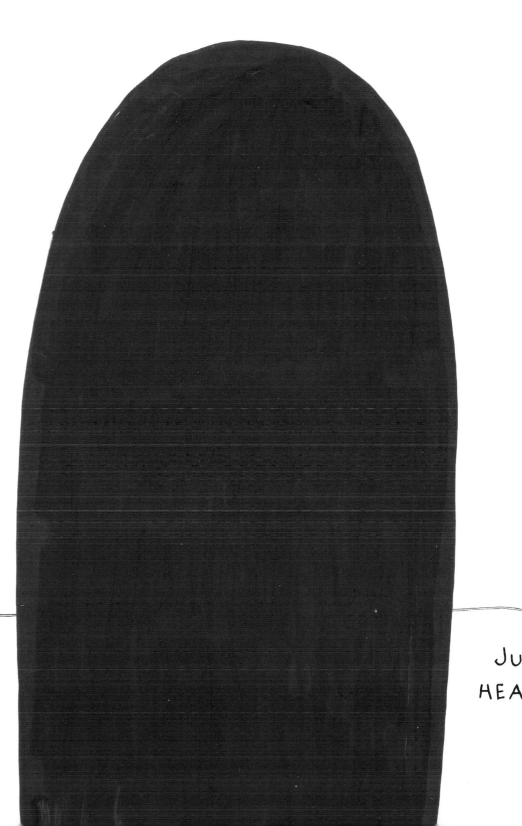

JUST SHAKE YOUR
HEAD REALLY HARD!

THAT WAS FUN, SPENDING
A LITTLE TIME WITH . . .
WELL, ON . . . YOU.

I THINK I MIGHT EVEN HAVE
GOTTEN USED TO THE PLACE.

WHOO . . . WHAT A TRIP . . . UH OH . . .

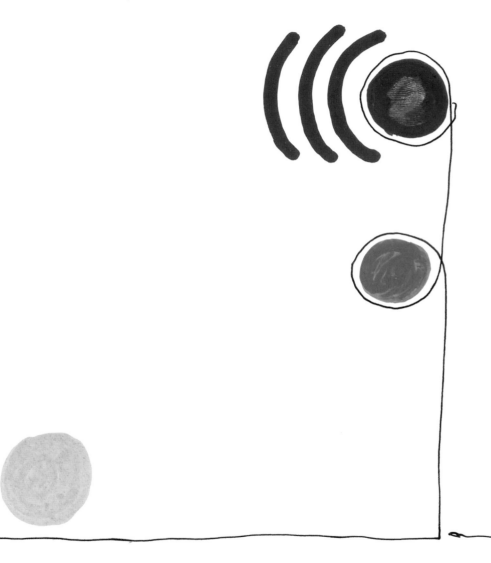

STOP! RED LIGHT!

ALL RIGHT, COUNT TO TEN AND . . .

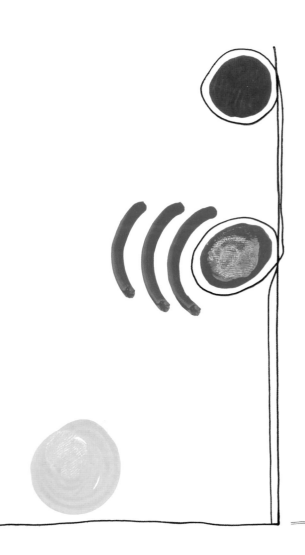

GREEN LIGHT! YOU CAN GO NOW.

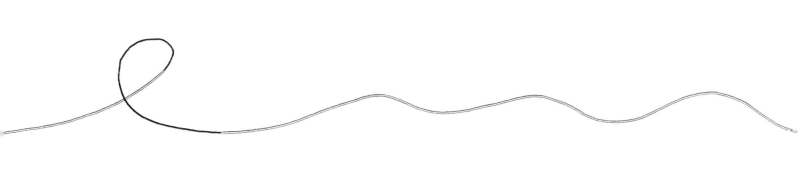

YOU CAN

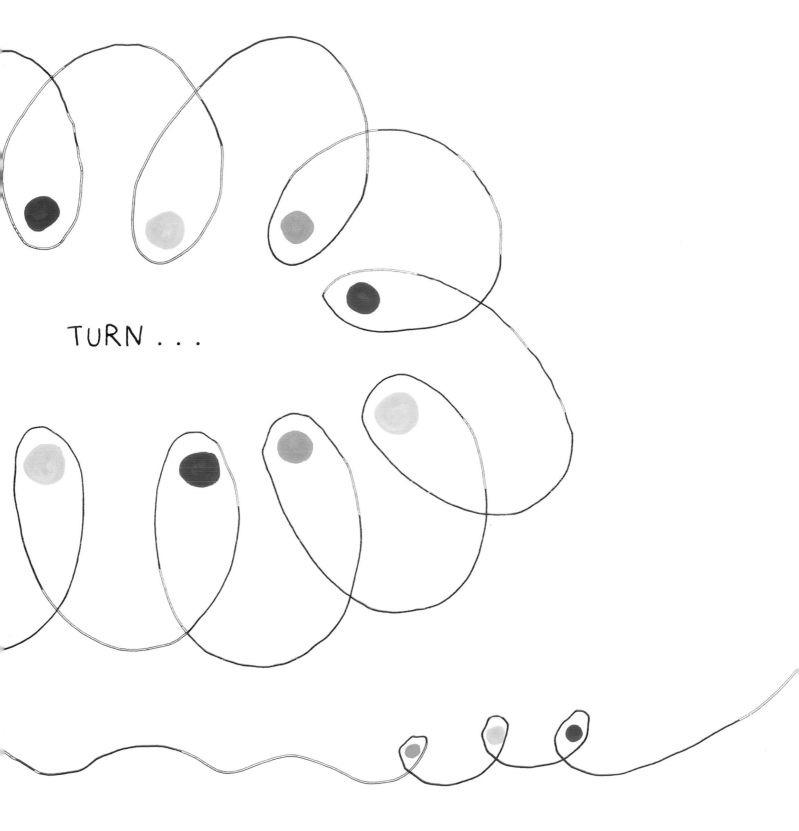

TURN . . .

YOU CAN RUN!

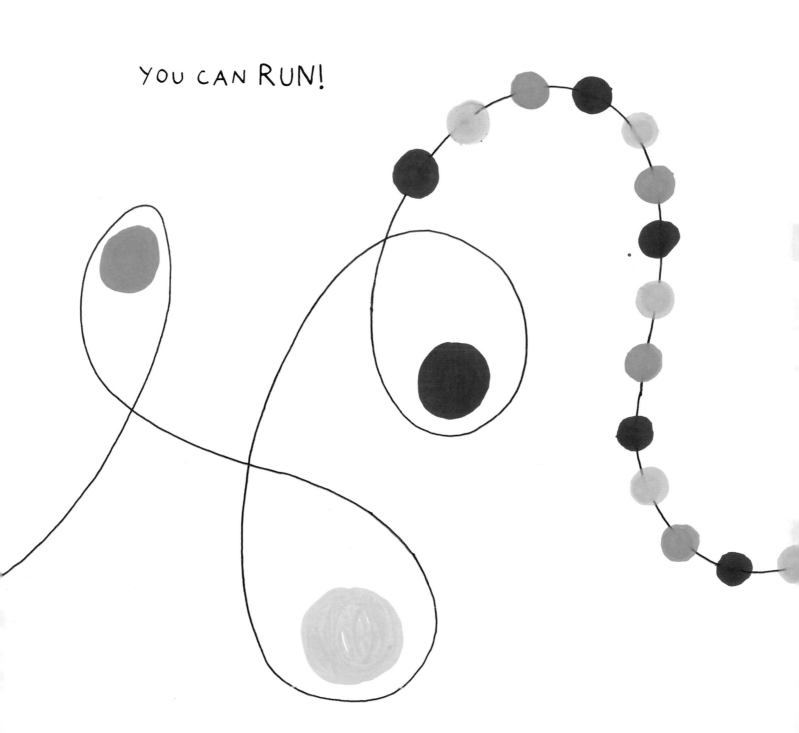

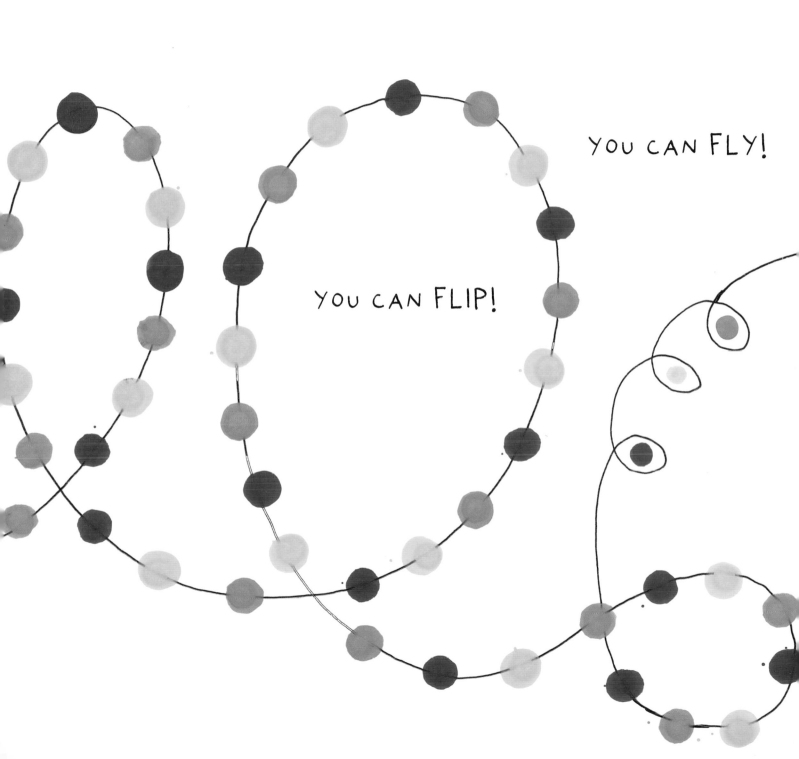

YOU CAN FLY!

YOU CAN FLIP!

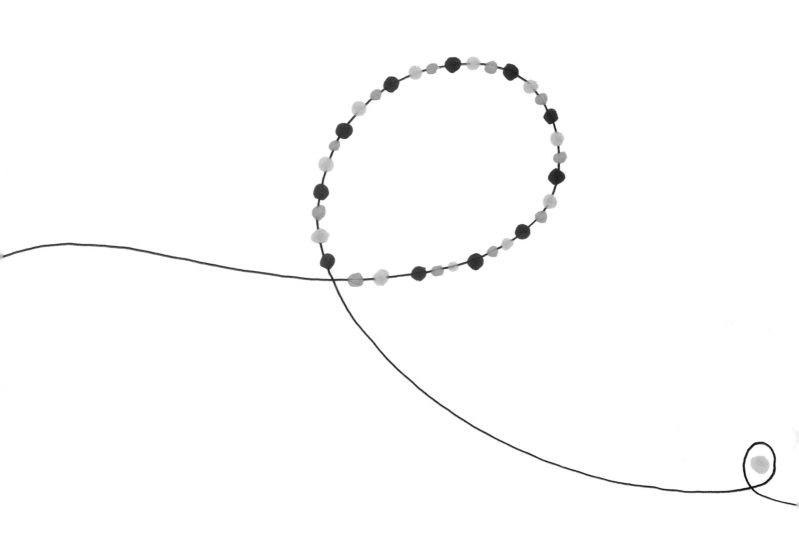

HEY!
DO YOU WANT TO COME BACK SOMETIME AND
PLAY SOME MORE?

First published in the United States of America in 2016 by Chronicle Books LLC.
Simultaneously published in France by Bayard Éditions under the title "Tu Joues?"

Text and illustration copyright © 2016 by Bayard Éditions.
Translation copyright © 2016 by Chronicle Books LLC.
All rights reserved. No part of this book may be reproduced in any form without written permission from the publisher.

Library of Congress Cataloging-in-Publication Data available.
ISBN 978-1-4521-5477-0

Manufactured in Malaysia by Tien Wah.

Translated by Christopher Franceschelli.
Original French edition design by Sandrine Granon.
Handprint/Chronicle Books edition design by Amelia Mack.
Typeset in Hervé Tullet Whimsy.
The illustrations in this book were rendered in paint.

10 9 8 7 6 5 4 3 2 1

Handprint Books
An imprint of Chronicle Books LLC
680 Second Street
San Francisco, California 94107

www.chroniclekids.com
www.chroniclebooks.com/letsplay
www.herve-tullet.com

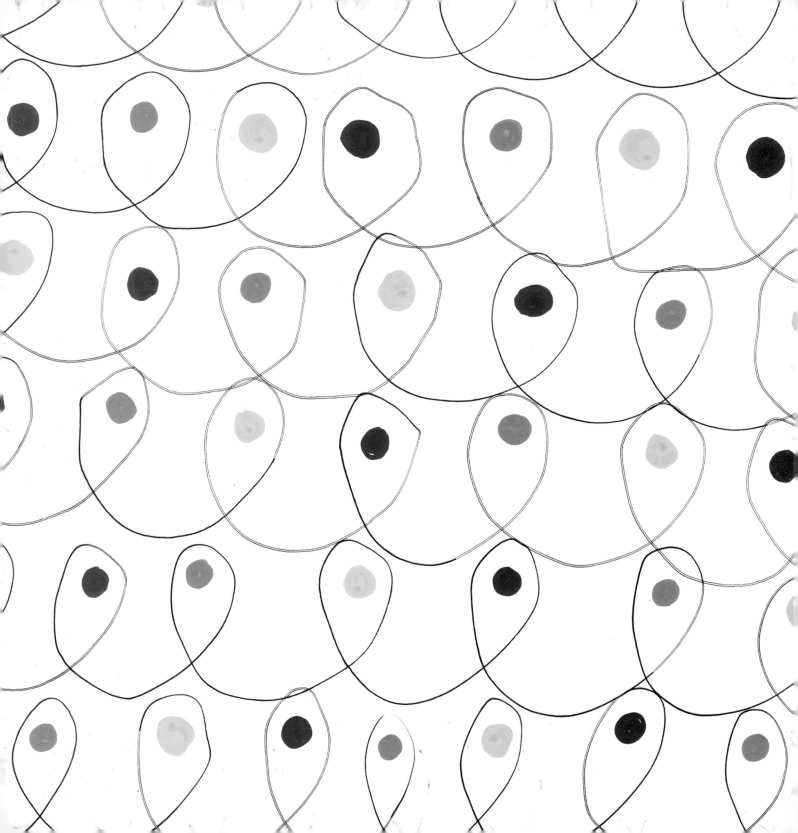